THE SPY FIVE
OPERATION
WISE DISGUISE

by Spencer Strange

with

Andrea Menotti — words

and

Kelly Kennedy — pictures

Scholastic Inc.

New York Toronto London Auckland Sydney
Mexico City New Delhi Hong Kong Buenos Aires

Visit the Spy Five web site at
www.scholastic.com/spyfive
Your new password is:
wiseguise

Stop by
and send the
Spy Five an
e-mail. We
love to hear
from you!

Use this password
to access a new
game!

ISBN 0-439-70354-9

Copyright © 2005 by Scholastic Inc.

Design: Julie Mullarkey Gnoy

12 11 10 9 8 7 6 5 4 3 2 1   5 6 7 8 9/0

Printed in the U.S.A.

First printing, March 2005

CHAPTERS

BASIC READING AND MATH
STANDARDIZED TEST

01) ⓐ ⓑ ⓒ ⓓ ⓔ
02) ⓐ ⓑ ⓒ ⓓ ⓔ
03) ⓐ ⓑ ⓒ ⓓ ⓔ
04) ⓐ ⓑ ⓒ ⓓ ⓔ
05) ⓐ ⓑ ⓒ ⓓ ⓔ
06) ⓐ ⓑ ⓒ ⓓ ⓔ
07) ⓐ ⓑ ⓒ ⓓ ⓔ
08) ⓐ ⓑ ⓒ ⓓ ⓔ
09) ⓐ ⓑ ⓒ ⓓ ⓔ
10) ⓐ ⓑ ⓒ ⓓ ⓔ
11) ⓐ ⓑ ⓒ ⓓ ⓔ
12) ⓐ ⓑ ⓒ ⓓ ⓔ
13) ⓐ ⓑ ⓒ ⓓ ⓔ
14) ⓐ ⓑ ⓒ ⓓ ⓔ
15) ⓐ ⓑ ⓒ ⓓ ⓔ
16) ⓐ ⓑ ⓒ ⓓ ⓔ
17) ⓐ ⓑ ⓒ ⓓ ⓔ
18) ⓐ ⓑ ⓒ ⓓ ⓔ
19) ⓐ ⓑ ⓒ ⓓ ⓔ
20) ⓐ ⓑ ⓒ ⓓ ⓔ
21) ⓐ ⓑ ⓒ ⓓ ⓔ
22) ⓐ ⓑ ⓒ ⓓ ⓔ
23) ⓐ ⓑ ⓒ ⓓ ⓔ
24) ⓐ ⓑ ⓒ ⓓ ⓔ
25) ⓐ ⓑ ⓒ ⓓ ⓔ

26) ⓐ ⓑ ⓒ ⓓ ⓔ
27) ⓐ ⓑ ⓒ ⓓ ⓔ
28) ⓐ ⓑ ⓒ ⓓ ⓔ
29) ⓐ ⓑ ⓒ ⓓ ⓔ
30) ⓐ ⓑ ⓒ ⓓ ⓔ
31) ⓐ ⓑ ⓒ ⓓ ⓔ
32) ⓐ ⓑ ⓒ ⓓ ⓔ
33) ⓐ ⓑ ⓒ ⓓ ⓔ
34) ⓐ ⓑ ⓒ ⓓ ⓔ
35) ⓐ ⓑ ⓒ ⓓ ⓔ
36) ⓐ ⓑ ⓒ ⓓ ⓔ
37) ⓐ ⓑ ⓒ ⓓ ⓔ
38) ⓐ ⓑ ⓒ ⓓ ⓔ
39) ⓐ ⓑ ⓒ ⓓ ⓔ
40) ⓐ ⓑ ⓒ ⓓ ⓔ
41) ⓐ ⓑ ⓒ ⓓ ⓔ
42) ⓐ ⓑ ⓒ ⓓ ⓔ
43) ⓐ ⓑ ⓒ ⓓ ⓔ
44) ⓐ ⓑ ⓒ ⓓ ⓔ
45) ⓐ ⓑ ⓒ ⓓ ⓔ
46) ⓐ ⓑ ⓒ ⓓ ⓔ
47) ⓐ ⓑ ⓒ ⓓ ⓔ
48) ⓐ ⓑ ⓒ ⓓ ⓔ
49) ⓐ ⓑ ⓒ ⓓ ⓔ
50) ⓐ ⓑ ⓒ ⓓ ⓔ

CHAPTER 1
WE GOT YOUR BACK, BLITZ

he stress level was VERY high at school all through the month of March because:

A) Principal Naulty was yelling even more than usual.

B) The statewide BRM test (which stands for Basic Reading and Math) was the second week of April.

C) The BRM was a super-important test that was going to decide who could go to the next grade...and who couldn't.

D) The BRM test was going to decide who lived and who died.

E) The BRM test was going to decide whether the world would end or not.

F) The BRM test was going to decide whether the sun would keep on shining.

G) All of the above

If you picked G, then congratulations. The dreaded BRM test was right around the corner, and let me tell you, the way the teachers and Mr. Naulty were acting, you'd think all of us were right on the edge of doom.

We'd been getting ready for the test all year long, and now the teachers were kicking it into high gear. That meant test prep, test prep, and—let's not forget—test prep.

People were starting to look like this:

I was definitely glad that the end was in sight. I was getting real tired of everyone talking about the test, and the teachers warning people that they were gonna fail if they didn't shape up, and all the stress around the whole thing. It was getting kind of nauseating.

I think maybe *that's* why Blitz got into his mess. Or at least, I think everybody being all stressed out helped turn Blitz's *little* mess into a big, crazy, out-of-control mess.

✳ ✳ ✳ ✳

Blitz's mess started one Friday at lunch. None of us were there for the actual moment when it all began, but right after it happened, Blitz came running over to me and Julian at our lunch table. He looked totally panicked.

"Guys," he said. "I'm in HUGE TROUBLE."

"What happened?"

"I stepped on Kyle Gordy's sneaker!" Blitz said, looking nervously toward the lunch line. "He was behind me in the lunch line, and they told us all to back up. And I stepped on his shoe!"

Julian and I looked at each other in disbelief. How could this be such a big deal?

"So?" I said.

"Whaddya mean, SO?" Blitz blasted back. "It left a BIG MARK. And his sneakers were BRAND-NEW! He said he was gonna BEAT ME UP after school!"

"WHOA! Hold on a second," Julian said. "Can't he just wipe off his shoe?"

"He tried!" Blitz said. "He spit on a napkin and everything. But it just got more smeared in!"

"*What* was on your shoe?" I asked.

"I don't know," Blitz said. "I must've stepped in something. Whatever it was, it wasn't coming off. And he's REAL MAD!"

"What's his *problem*?" I said. "Shoes get dirty. It's a fact of life!"

"Tell that to *him*!" Blitz said. "I'm DEAD MEAT, guys!"

Sheesh. It seemed so ridiculous that someone would get so mad over a stupid mark on a stupid sneaker. But I'm sorry to say, that's how it is at my school. People make a big deal about clothes, especially big-name labels, and *especially* sneakers.

At my old school in Maryland, guys didn't care that much about how their sneakers looked. But here in New York City, it's a different story. Guys *really* care about having the latest, newest, most spotless sneakers. It's a major deal. So I knew that's where Kyle was coming from.

"Okay, let's be reasonable here," I said. "Kyle just needs to use some kind of cleaner. Maybe we can get something from the kitchen."

We all looked toward the kitchen. It was a Friday, so Ursula had her smoothie stand set up right near the lunch line. She'd been doing that every Friday since last fall (after we teamed up with the cafeteria manager in *Operation Fowl Play*). The cafeteria ladies always helped Ursula out with the stand, so we knew she had an inside track to the kitchen supplies.

We all had the same thought.

"Maybe Ursula can hook us up," Julian said.

So we all headed over to smoothie central to see if Ursula could help.

* * * *

"Can't you see I'm trying to run a business?" Ursula asked when the three of us crowded behind the stand to talk to her.

"We have a *situation*," I said, quickly explaining what Blitz had done.

"*What* was on your shoe?" Ursula asked, looking down at Blitz's feet with raised eyebrows.

"I don't know," Blitz said, holding up his hands in desperation. "But can you get the cafeteria ladies to give us some cleaner?"

Ursula thought for a second.

"I wouldn't trust this school's cleaning supplies. You could end up burning a *hole* through that sneaker," Ursula said, reaching for her bag underneath the stand. "Fortunately, I think *I* have the answer for you."

"You carry *cleaners* around?" Julian asked in disbelief.

"No," Ursula said. "But lucky for you, I happen to have a *moist towelette.*"

And she proudly handed Blitz one of those hand-wipe things.

"You think *this* is gonna get that mark off?" Blitz asked.

"Unless you had toxic waste on your shoe, yes, I think so," Ursula said. "Now if you'll excuse me, I have to get back to my smoothies."

And so we thanked Ursula and headed back to our table.

✻ ✻ ✻ ✻

"I'm *not* walking up to Kyle Gordy and offering him a *moist towelette,*" Blitz said, shaking his head. "That's like a *suicide* mission."

"He won't lay a finger on you," Julian said. "He knows he'd get suspended if he started a fight in school."

"But what if he doesn't *care* about getting suspended?" Blitz asked.

"He *cares,*" Julian said. "He knows if you get suspended too many times, you get sent to jail."

"You *do?*" Blitz and I both asked.

"Well, not exactly jail. It's some kind of school that's *like* jail," Julian said. "My cousin told me about it. He said it's like detention all—"

But Julian couldn't finish, because suddenly we heard...

And we turned and saw Kyle charging toward us with a furious look on his face. His friends Eddie and Jake were with him. All three of them were bad-news characters.

"THIS IS THE KID WHO WRECKED MY SNEAKER," Kyle announced to his friends, pointing at Blitz.

He didn't actually say "kid" or "wrecked," you know. He said MUCH worse stuff. I'm just being decent.

"It was an *accident*, okay?" Julian said with a very serious face. "Give him a chance to fix it."

And Blitz stepped forward.

"This might work if you want to try it," he said in a small voice, holding out the moist towelette with a wince.

Kyle took the moist towelette and wrinkled his nose at it like he was holding a packet of horse manure. We all wondered what exactly he was going to do.

"*You* clean my shoe," Kyle said, handing the moist towelette back to Blitz. "You made the mess. You clean it up."

Blitz looked at me and Julian, and we both shrugged. We weren't exactly in a position to argue.

So Blitz unwrapped the little towel thing and started wiping off Kyle's shoe.

But pretty soon it was clear that the sneaker mark wasn't going anywhere. And I mean AN-Y-WHERE.

And Blitz *really* tried, too. He finally stood up in defeat.

"I think we need a better cleaner," he said.

"And *you* need to learn to STAY OUT OF PEOPLE'S WAY and OFF OF PEOPLE'S PROPERTY," Kyle said, pointing his finger in Blitz's face.

"Hey," Julian said, stepping forward.

But Kyle just ignored Julian.

"You don't even want to *know* how much these shoes cost," Kyle said, leaning even closer to Blitz. "I should make you buy me new ones, Yellowhead."

"HEY," Julian said again, this time louder.

"I'm not talking to *you*," Kyle said to Julian. "I'm talking to *him*. And he knows he better watch his back. 'Cause I'm not kidding. And I don't care *whose* friend he is."

And then Kyle turned to Blitz one last time and added:

"I'll see *you* after school, Yellowhead."

And with one last "you-better-watch-out" look, Kyle and his friends walked off.

"See?" Blitz said, looking at both of us. "This is BAD."

"Don't panic," Julian said, looking as serious as I'd ever seen him. "We got your back."

✳ ✳ ✳ ✳

We talked about the whole sneaker situation with Ursula and Anika after lunch in the school yard.

"The moist towelette didn't work?" Ursula asked.

"Nope," I said. "And Kyle told Blitz to 'watch his back.'"

"HE CAN'T BEAT UP BLITZ!" Ursula blasted out, really loud. "He can get suspended for that!"

"That's why he said he was gonna beat me up *after* school," Blitz said anxiously. "They can't suspend you for *that*, can they?"

"But he's threatening you *during* school," Anika insisted.

"We should tell Miss Pryor," Ursula said. "*She'll* help."

"But he'll get even madder if he gets in trouble!" Blitz protested. "Then he'll *definitely* be out to get me!"

Ursula thought for a second.

"Well, it's *possible* that we can handle this ourselves. I have connections in the cleaning industry, you know."

"You do?" we all asked.

"Yeah. My uncle owns a dry-cleaning business," Ursula explained. "He's a complete *magician* when it comes to stains. I bet he'll have some kind of cleaner we can use to make that sneaker look good as new."

"REALLY?" Blitz asked, looking totally grateful.

"Yeah," Ursula said. "I'll stop by his store this afternoon and see what I can round up. I'm sure he'll have *something*."

"And in the meantime, I'll keep an ear out for any news about Kyle's plans for after school," Anika said. "I know some of his friends. Maybe I can get them to talk him out of anything stupid."

"And *we'll* walk home with you," Julian said to Blitz, nodding to me.

"Hopefully Kyle will just forget about the whole thing," I said.

"He didn't *seem* like he was gonna forget," Blitz said doubtfully. "And every time he looks at his shoe, he's gonna remember."

Blitz shook his head and looked down at the pavement.

"This is such a stupid mess," he mumbled. "I can't *believe* this is happening to me."

"He's just trying to scare you," Julian said. "He's not gonna hurt you."

"You heard what he said," Blitz insisted. "He said he was gonna—"

"And *I* said he's NOT," Julian interrupted. "Like I said: We got your back, Blitz. You can count on that."

CHAPTER 2
THE NOT-SO-GREAT ESCAPE

Later that afternoon, I ran into Anika in the hall. Her face looked very worried.

"Bad news, Spencer," she said. "Word is, Kyle's definitely gonna jump Blitz after school."

"He *is*?" I asked.

"Yup," she said. "He's gonna be waiting outside the main doors with his friends, and they're gonna follow Blitz down the block."

"Does Blitz know?" I asked.

"I already warned him," Anika said. "I told him I thought we should tell a teacher or *somebody*, but he kept saying how that would make everything even worse than it already was. I think he's scared out of his mind."

"We'll look out for him till this whole thing blows over," I said.

"Whenever *that* might be," Anika said.

"I can't believe it's such a big deal," I said. "It's just a stupid sneaker. I get marks on my sneakers, like, every *day*."

"If you ask me, Kyle's just looking for somebody to beat up on," Anika said. "I've known him since elementary school, and he's always been like that."

I shook my head.

"Why do people like Kyle Gordy have to *exist*?" I asked.

"Ya got me," Anika said. "Life's too short to be hating like that."

LIFE'S TOO SHORT TO BE HATING LIKE THAT.

"Anyway," I said. "I'll talk to Julian and Blitz, and we'll figure out a plan for today after school. There's gotta be some way we can slip past Kyle."

"Sounds good," Anika said. "Let me know if I can help."

* * * *

That afternoon I met up with Julian and Blitz in the hall before last period.

"Did you HEAR?" Blitz asked, his eyes enormous. "They're gonna be waiting outside the main doors!"

"Yeah, Anika told me," I said.

"I heard, too," Julian said. "We'll help you get home safe. Don't worry."

"Do you think we should hide out in the library till they leave?" Blitz asked. "That's what I was thinking."

"Nah," Julian said. "We don't know how long they're gonna stick around. It's better to leave right away. Then we can use the crowd for cover."

"But maybe they'll only stay five *minutes* or something," Blitz argued.

"I've seen Kyle and those guys hanging out on the corner an *hour* after school," Julian said. "Nothing better to do, I guess."

"And remember, we can only stay in the library till three o'clock on Fridays," I added.

If we still had Homework Club after school, we could've stayed there, but that got cancelled last month. (The teacher who ran it got fed up because none of us were actually getting our homework done.) So, since we don't have Homework Club, we either hang out in the library or just go straight home after school.

"We can't hang out here," Julian insisted. "We gotta leave when the whole school is emptying out, so we can blend in with the crowd. The *last* thing we need is to run into Kyle on an empty street."

Blitz kind of shuddered.

"But how are we supposed to slip out?" Blitz asked anxiously. "They're gonna be right there!"

Julian looked around and leaned in closer.

"We'll go out the gym doors," he said.

"How are we gonna get into the *gym*?" Blitz asked in despair.

"*Yeah*," I said, because we all knew the gym was always locked after school.

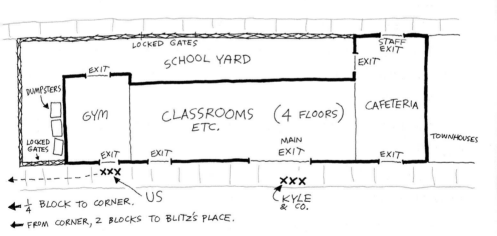

"I talked to Kelvin," Julian said, referring to a janitor we knew pretty well from some operations we did earlier in the year. "He said he'd keep the gym open for us."

"How'd you swing *that*?" I asked, totally amazed.

"I just told him, straight up, we didn't want to walk past some guys who were trying to cause trouble," Julian said with a shrug. "He said he'd keep the door unlocked. He said he's always on the ground floor around that time anyway."

Since the gym exit was pretty far from the main exit, and closer to Blitz's place (which, luckily, was really close to school), it seemed like the perfect plan. We'd only have to walk a short way, and then we could turn the corner and be completely out of sight.

"Thanks," Blitz said, looking relieved.

"No problem," Julian said. "We'll come get you in your homeroom right after school. Be ready to go right when the bell rings, okay?"

"Okay," Blitz said.

He looked *really* grateful.

✳ ✳ ✳ ✳

At the end of the day, Julian and I dashed over to Blitz's homeroom. As planned, he was ready to go.

We slipped down the hall toward the small stairwell that led to the side of the building where the gym was. No one was there, since that stairwell usually led to a dead end.

After we ran down the steps, we found Kelvin mopping out one of the bathrooms on the ground floor.

"Hello, kiddos," Kelvin said cheerfully.

"Is the gym open?" Julian asked urgently.

"Yep, just finished in there," Kelvin said. "Door's unlocked."

"Thanks," we all said, making a quick turn into the gym.

"Are you sure you kids are okay?" he asked. "Because—"

But we didn't wait to hear the rest.

"Yes!" we called back, already charging across the basketball court.

Once we'd made our way across the gym to the door that opened onto the street, Julian quickly peeked out to see if Kyle and his friends were at the main exit (which was farther up the block).

I could tell they were there, because Julian quickly ducked back inside.

Kyle and company

"They're there?" Blitz asked.

"Yup," Julian nodded with a wince. "All three of 'em."

Blitz looked even paler than usual. I didn't even think that was *possible*.

"They didn't see you, did they?" I asked.

"Nope," Julian said. "They're watching the main exit. Let's just wait a couple seconds till the block fills up, then go."

And so we waited as kids poured out of the main exit and headed down the block, past our door. Pretty soon, the sidewalk was packed, and it looked like we had plenty of cover.

"When I give the word, we're gonna walk out," Julian said to Blitz. "*Walk*, not run, you got it?"

Blitz nodded.

"Just look normal, like part of the crowd," I added. "You don't want to attract any attention. You have lots of cover, so just stay cool."

"Okay," Blitz said.

"And don't look where Kyle is. Just keep walking," Julian said. "No eye contact with Kyle. That would be *it*. You got it?"

"Got it," Blitz said.

So, just when the crowd was getting really thick, we quickly stepped out the door and joined it.

"This is when I wish I had eyes in the back of my head," Julian muttered as we walked along with the crowd, trying to act as normal as possible.

us

Kyle and buddies

We were almost to the end of the block when we heard...

And there was Anika, rushing toward us with a four-alarm-fire face.

"*Run, guys!*" she yelled. "They're coming! Behind you!"

Julian and I looked at each other in disbelief. *What* had gone wrong? And where had Anika come from? But there was no time to wonder about that.

"COME ON!" Julian said. "RUN!"

And the three of us started to run. And that's when we heard:

"HEY, YELLOWHEAD!"

I turned quickly and saw that we had almost half a block on Kyle and company, so I knew we just had to run fast to keep our lead. Blitz turned to look, too, but that really slowed him down.

"Don't look back!" Julian shouted to Blitz. "Just GO!"

So we tore around the corner and headed up the block toward Blitz's place.

Julian could run really fast, and so could I, but unfortunately, Blitz was *really* slow. We had to go a lot slower than normal to stay with him.

But lucky for us, Kyle and his friends weren't exactly speed demons. (Kyle's kind of a fatso, and his friends are, too.)

"Gimme your backpack," Julian said, grabbing Blitz's bag and slinging it over his shoulder next to his own. "Man! What do you *have* in here?"

Blitz just shrugged, too out of breath to answer.

After that, we went a lot faster. Pretty soon we were at Blitz's building, and Blitz was digging frantically through his coat pockets looking for his keys. Finally he realized they weren't even in there.

"They're in my bag!" he said, pointing to the backpack.

Immediately Julian dropped the bag on the ground, and Blitz started digging through it. I couldn't *believe* how much junk he had in there. Neither could Julian.

"Come on, Blitz!" Julian said. "They're getting closer!"

Finally Blitz pulled out his keys and ran up to the door.

"My STUFF!" he shouted.

"We'll get it!" Julian shouted. "Just OPEN THE DOOR!"

Julian and I grabbed Blitz's stuff and scrambled to the door. We burst inside, slammed the door behind us, and piled up the steps just in time to see Kyle and his friends plaster themselves against the door window.

"NEXT TIME, YELLOWHEAD!"
"WE KNOW WHERE YOU LIVE!"
"SEE YOU MONDAY!"

They said all kinds of stuff like that and WORSE, let me tell you. But we just kept running up the stairs.

Once we were inside Blitz's apartment, we all collapsed on the couch, totally out of breath.

"How did they SEE us?" Julian asked. "There were, like, five hundred *thousand* other kids on that block!"

Okay, five hundred thousand was a bit of an exaggeration. But there were at least a couple *hundred*.

"I don't know," I said with a shrug. "I thought we were home free."

"Maybe they got an overhead view," Blitz said, still trying to catch his breath. "Maybe they stood on a lamppost or something."

"The street *does* go downhill," Julian agreed. "So I guess they could've seen us if they looked over the crowd."

"And Blitz is one of the only 'yellowheads' in the entire school," I added. "So he'd be pretty easy to spot."

"And *you're* a yellowhead, too," Julian said, pointing at my head.

"My hair's light *brown*," I argued.

"Close enough," Julian said.

Julian was right—there weren't too many yellowheads or *almost* yellowheads at my school. Most kids in my school had brown or black hair.

"Anyway," Julian said, changing the subject. "Good thing Anika was there, or they definitely would've caught up to us."

"Yeah, good thing," Blitz agreed, walking over to the window and peeking out. "They're still down there, you know."

Julian and I joined Blitz at the window. Down below, Kyle and his friends were shouting all sorts of stuff that would've been bleeped if it was on TV.

"We'll just hang out here till they go," I said, taking a seat on the couch.

"Good thing it's Friday," Blitz said.

"No kidding," Julian agreed.

At least we had the whole weekend to figure out what to do next.

CHAPTER 3
TWO GOOD TRICKS

T hat night, I got an e-mail from Anika asking if we'd all gotten home okay. She said she'd made a point of standing on the corner after school so she could watch us and get help if anything bad happened. I told her that we'd all managed to escape, and that I was coming up with a plan for Monday.

But I have to say, coming up with a plan was not exactly a cinch. I thought about the whole crazy problem for a while. Basically, we needed some kind of solution that would tide us over till one of the following things happened:

A) Ursula came through with the sneaker cleaner.

B) Kyle forgot about the whole thing.

C) Kyle found someone else to pick on.

D) Blitz became an Olympic sprinter and champion kick-boxing ninja.

E) Kyle was deported to Mars.

F) All of the above

Hopefully *some* kind of happily-ever-after ending would happen soon. But until then, we had to figure out how to help Blitz get home every day in one piece.

So, on Saturday morning, I got out some books I have on spy tactics and read up on the two areas I knew we had to focus on—escape and disguise. As usual, Mom kept trying to bother me with various ridiculous things the entire morning. But fortunately I was still able to get stuff done.

Sometimes I'm amazed I can get *anything* done at home.

Anyway, after I came up with my ideas, I called up both Blitz and Julian and got them to meet me at the 91st Street garden in Riverside Park at 1:00. I figured we could talk about our options and come up with a plan.

✳ ✳ ✳ ✳

Once Julian and Blitz had both arrived at the park, I laid out the options for them.

Option #1:
The Quick-Change Disguise

1) Blitz walks past Kyle and company in his coat and backpack right before school ends.

2) Blitz goes into homeroom and changes coat and backpack and hides yellow hair under a hat. Leaves extra stuff in homeroom.

3) Blitz slips out gym exit. But now, because his appearance has changed completely, Kyle can't pick him out of the crowd.

Option #2: The Decoy

1) We buy a blond shaggy wig and someone wears Blitz's coat (someone who can run really FAST).

Either Spencer or Julian could be the decoy.

2) The decoy comes out the gym exit and walks slowly till he's sure that Kyle and company see him (from the back only). When the decoy knows he's been spotted, he runs.

decoy

3) The decoy runs to a "safe house," somewhere in the opposite direction from Blitz's place, like Ursula's place.

4) After Kyle and company go running after the decoy, Blitz slips out the door and walks home.

"Ooh," Julian said with a grin. "I wanna be the decoy! I could outrun those guys *any* day."

"That would be an awesome trick to pull on 'em," Blitz nodded. "But where are we gonna get a wig?"

"Well," I said, turning my notebook to the next page, "I checked online, and there are a couple of costume shops downtown where they sell wigs. But they're all like..."

I winced.

"...twenty or thirty *bucks*."

The other guys winced, too.

"Man, that's *steep*," Julian agreed.

"Maybe we could pool our money together or something," I continued. "If we each gave a couple bucks, we could get one of the cheaper wigs. Seems like it's worth it, since the yellow hair is our Achilles' heel."

I could tell from the looks on Julian and Blitz's faces that they had no idea what an Achilles' heel was. Guess they hadn't studied any Greek mythology in fifth grade like I had. So I explained.

"Achilles was this ancient Greek guy whose only weak spot was his heel. Otherwise he was impossible to kill, like a god," I explained, pointing to my heel. "So our weak spot is the yellow hair, since that's what makes Blitz easy to spot in a crowd."

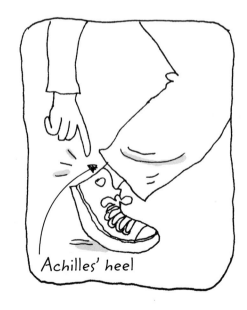

Achilles' heel

"Got it," Blitz nodded. "I think we should get the wig. But you guys shouldn't have to spend your money. I have twenty-six bucks."

"You *do?*" Julian and I both said.

"Yup," Blitz nodded. "I've been saving up for robot parts."

"You're building a *robot?*" I asked.

"I'm actually building a couple of 'em," Blitz said. "Just little ones. But I can put the robots on hold. Saving my neck is a lot more important."

"Twenty-six whole bucks down the drain for a wig?" Julian said, shaking his head. "That's not right."

I felt bad, too. It didn't seem right for Blitz to have to break the bank like that, all because of a deadbeat like Kyle.

"We can just do the quick-change option," I said. "It might seem simple, but it really works. We can test it out to prove it—"

"*I* think we should do the wig," Blitz insisted. "It's okay to spend the money. I'll earn it again, as long as I keep emptying the dishwasher."

And so it was settled. We decided to head downtown to buy the wig right away.

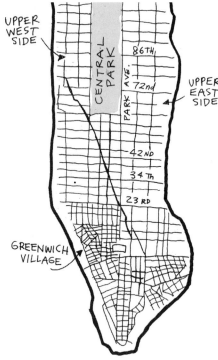

CHAPTER 4
A GREAT WIG DEAL

It was actually kind of hard to find the costume shop. It was in this part of town called Greenwich Village, which people call "the Village" for short. Down there, the streets go every which way instead of in a grid like in our part of town. And most of the streets have names instead of numbers, so you pretty much have to use a map to find your street (or know where you're going).

But eventually, after a lot of wrong turns, we found the place: Masquerade Market.

We went inside and started looking around. There were tons of cool masks, hats, and wigs. We tried a bunch of them on.

But then the fun came crashing to a halt, because suddenly we had to deal with...

MR. SUSPICIOUS.

"May I help you, boys?" he asked in a not-very-helpful voice.

He looked convinced that we were there to steal something, or break something, or cause some other kind of trouble. Annoying.

"We're here to buy a wig," I said, stepping forward.

"A wig like his hair," Julian said, pointing to Blitz's head.

"Wigs like that are *very expensive*, you know," Mr. Suspicious said.

"We know," Blitz said, and then, sounding very serious, he added: "We have twenty-six dollars."

Blitz opened his wallet and pulled out a wad of cash. And suddenly, Mr. Suspicious turned into Mr. All Business.

"All right then," he said. "Let me show you our collection."

Mr. All Business walked us over to a counter covered in foam heads with wigs on them. All the faces had lipstick on and looked like ladies.

"Don't you have any *guy's* wigs?" Julian asked.

"The short wigs can be worn by either ladies OR gentlemen," Mr. All Business said with a sniff, moving forward several of the short, blond wigs.

"That one!" Blitz said, pointing to one of the shaggier heads. "That's my hair!"

"Try it on!" I said to Julian.

Blitz hair

So Julian tried the wig on. It was really funny looking at Julian with Blitz's hair. It was definitely just the right color and style. Julian just kept staring at himself in the mirror with a funny look on his face.

"I look like a girl," Julian said, and then he thought for a second and added: "No offense, Blitz. I just mean how it looks on *me*."

"You can wear a hat on top of it," I said. "So they'll only see the hair in the back. That's all we really want them to see anyway. And the hat'll help the wig stay on, too."

After I said *that*, Mr. All Business suddenly became Mr. Nosy.

"Can I ask why exactly you need a wig?" Mr. Nosy asked.

We all looked at one another, trying to figure out who was going to explain and what exactly he was going to say.

"It's a school thing," I finally said. "An after-school project."

"Oh," Mr. Nosy said. "Drama club?"

"Yes," Blitz and Julian both said at the same time.

"Yeah, it's drama, all right," I added.

I wasn't lying, after all—this was definitely one of the most dramatic things we'd done all year!

"Okay," Mr. Nosy said. "Shall we ring this up, then?"

So Julian took off the wig, and we all went to the register.

"How much is it?" Blitz asked.

Julian looked at the tag on the inside of the wig.

"Whoa!" Julian said. "It's $29.99!"

"No way!" Blitz said, looking disappointed.

And that's when I spotted the sale sign on the wall.

"Hey, look!" I said, pointing to the sign. "The wigs are on sale!"

"I was just about to mention that," Mr. Nosy said.

A likely story!

And so Blitz paid for the wig (he had *just* enough!), and we were out of there.

✳ ✳ ✳ ✳

On the way back uptown on the subway, I realized I'd forgotten to show the guys a cool thing I'd brought from my spy gear collection.

"Hey, Julian," I said. "Remember when we were trying to slip past Kyle on Friday, and you said you wished you had eyes in the back of your head?"

"Yeah," Julian said, looking confused.

"Well, here's the next best thing," I said, handing Julian my pair of rearview glasses. "Rearview glasses. Try 'em on."

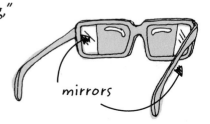

mirrors

"Sweet!" Julian said, once he'd put on the glasses. "I can see stuff behind me!"

"Lemme try!" Blitz said.

So Julian handed the glasses to Blitz.

"Cool!" Blitz said, turning his head away from us. "I can see you guys!"

"When you're walking out of school, you can wear these," I said to Blitz. "So you'll know if anyone's sneaking up behind you."

"Good idea," Julian said.

"I think *Julian* should wear them," Blitz insisted. "Since he's the one who's putting himself on the line, being the decoy and all."

"I'll be okay," Julian said. "You wear 'em."

"No, *you!*" Blitz said.

"We'll figure it out," I said.

Maybe there was some way I could buy another pair....

CHAPTER 5
THE DECOY PLOY

ut as it turned out, on Monday morning before school, Blitz had a surprise:

Four extra pairs of rearview glasses!

rearview glasses

"I made 'em," Blitz explained. "I bought some little plastic mirrors and taped them to the sides of these sunglasses. Easy!"

"Where'd you get all the glasses?" I asked.

"Well, *I* had two pairs because I thought I lost mine last summer," Blitz said. "But then I found 'em after I got a new pair. And my mom had some old broken ones lying around, so I fixed 'em up and made two pairs for the girls."

"Nice," I said.

Right then, Ursula walked in.

"We're in luck, guys," she said excitedly. "My uncle's store carries the best sneaker cleaner on the *planet!*"

"Really?!" we all said.

"Yup," she said. "Makes sneakers look good as new."

Blitz's eyes got huge and his mouth dropped open.

"THANK YOU!" he said. "You're a LIFESAVER!"

Blitz looked like he was about ready to give Ursula a great big bear hug. Okay, maybe not. But then came the bad news.

"Well," Ursula said, "I haven't exactly saved you *yet*. The sneaker cleaner's out of stock right now. But my uncle said he'd order more, and he should get it real soon."

Everyone's face fell.

"How long will it take?" Blitz asked, looking really disappointed.

"I don't know," Ursula said. "Two days maybe?"

We all winced. Two days was a long time to have Kyle breathing down our necks.

"Well, at least we didn't buy the wig for nothing," Julian said.

"YOU BOUGHT A *WIG*?!" Ursula blasted out.

"SHHHH!" we all said.

"WHAT?" said another voice from behind us. "You bought a *wig*?"

We all turned to see Anika walking in right then.

"Yeah," Blitz said. "For the decoy ploy."

"The WHAT?" Ursula and Anika asked at the same time.

So we brought the girls up to speed on the plan. They seemed like they were on board with everything till I mentioned to Ursula that we wanted to use her apartment as a safe house.

"Why does it have to be *my* place?" she asked.

"Because your place is in the opposite direction from Blitz's place, and it's really close to school," I explained. "It's the absolute *perfect* location."

"And I'll run so fast, they won't even know which building I went into," Julian said. "I'll be *miles* ahead of 'em."

"And Julian would only have to be there for a little while, like ten minutes," I explained. "Then, when the coast was clear, after Blitz got home safe, I'd come get him."

Ursula looked really uncomfortable.

"I don't think it's a good idea, guys," she said.

"Why not?" I asked.

She shrugged.

"Are your parents strict about having people over?" Anika asked.

"No," Ursula said. "It's just *weird* to have someone over. My grandmother's there and...*stuff*."

"What's the problem with that?" Blitz asked.

Ursula just shrugged and wouldn't say anything more.

"Well, then Julian could just wait in the hall," I suggested.

"Yeah," Julian agreed.

Ursula thought for a second.

"Okay," she said finally. "But give me a head start so I can be there first. I'll wait at the door and open it for you. Then we'll hang out in the hall till Spencer shows up."

"Fine by me," Julian said.

"Thanks, Ursula," Blitz said.

"Yeah," everyone agreed.

I could tell Ursula was kind of pleased to be thanked by everyone.

Anyway, after that, Blitz showed the girls the glasses he'd made.

"Cool!" Ursula said, trying hers on.

"These'll come in real handy," Anika said. "They're perfect for watching our backs!"

"Exactly," I nodded.

COOL!

"We still have about five minutes till school starts," Julian said. "You guys wanna go outside and try using these things? Maybe do a quick test run of the decoy plan?"

"What if Kyle sees us?" Blitz asked.

"You think that boy gets to school on time?" Anika asked. "No way."

"And besides," I pointed out, "we can use the street *behind* the school. No one's ever there."

"Yeah," Julian agreed. "Let's go."

So we all headed downstairs.

✳   ✳   ✳   ✳

Once we were outside, we all put on our rearview glasses and tried walking around in them and checking out the view.

Then Julian even put on the Blitz wig and baseball cap, which the girls thought was really funny.

"Ooh, check out Julian as a blond!" Anika said. "Nice look!"

"Whatever," Julian said, putting on Blitz's coat, which just barely fit him. "Do I look like Blitz from the back?"

Julian turned around and stood next to Blitz.

"Yup," we all agreed.

"Good," Julian said. "And these glasses are perfect, 'cause that way I never have to turn to face those guys."

"Which is good, 'cause you definitely don't look *anything* like Blitz from the front," Ursula pointed out.

"Exactly," Julian said. "I'll just step out the gym exit and walk slowly till they spot me, then I'll make a break for it."

"And I'll stand on the corner," Anika said. "Just like I did on Friday. I'll watch for Julian and Kyle and those guys, and I'll go tell Spencer and Blitz when the coast is clear."

"You think we can use the gym exit again?" I asked Julian.

"Shouldn't be a problem," Julian said. "I'll just check with Kelvin."

"GUYS!" Ursula said suddenly, checking her watch. "School starts in ONE minute!"

"Oops," Blitz said.

Julian yanked off the wig and hat, and we all ran back inside.

* * * *

That day after lunch, we all met in the school yard. As usual, Kyle and his friends were playing basketball on their own personal court (because no one else dared play there).

We made sure to stay in a part of the school yard where they couldn't see us, just to make sure they wouldn't decide to come over and cause trouble.

"I talked to Kelvin," Julian said. "And we're all set with the gym exit."

"Perfect," I said, pulling out my notebook. "I sketched out the plan."

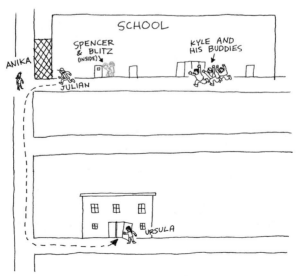

"Are we sure Kyle's still out to get Blitz?" Ursula asked. "Maybe he's moved on to some other victim by now."

"Um, 'fraid not," Anika said with a wince. "I've been asking around, and it sounds like they're definitely planning a repeat performance today after school. I guess it's kind of a pride thing since they failed on Friday."

Blitz took a deep breath.

"I know," Blitz said. "They were saying nasty stuff to me in the hall."

"Don't worry," Julian said to Blitz. "We got it covered."

"Kyle's gonna have to get used to being disappointed," I said. "'Cause this plan we worked out is totally *solid*."

"It *is* a very cool plan," Anika agreed. "I've never done anything like this in my life!"

"Me neither," I said, and Julian and Blitz agreed.

Ursula didn't chime in, though. Her forehead got all wrinkly.

"But guys," she said, "I've been thinking. Why do we have to go through all this trouble? Couldn't we just tell Kyle that we have a sneaker cleaner coming, and that he should just hold tight till it gets here? I'll tell him if you want."

"You want to *talk* to him?" Blitz asked.

"You think he'd be *reasonable*?" Julian asked with raised eyebrows.

"Why not?" Ursula asked. "It would be like a negotiation. I could handle it. Blitz could be my first client."

"Your first *client*?" Blitz asked.

"Yes," Ursula nodded. "Didn't you know I'm an official member of Future Lawyers of America?"

And Ursula reached into her bag, pulled out her wallet, took out a card, and held it up for us to see.

"It's FLA for short," Ursula added proudly.

We all looked at one another with wide eyes, trying not to crack up. But we weren't very good actors, because Ursula could tell immediately what we all thought.

"What?" Ursula asked defensively. "What's wrong with being a member of FLA?"

"Nothing," we all said quickly.

"And what's wrong with negotiating?" she asked. "I could just walk up to Kyle and say that we'd resolve his complaint within the week by removing his sneaker stain. And in the meantime, he would need to agree to leave Blitz alone. And if he didn't agree to that, we wouldn't fix his sneaker. Fair and square."

I could only imagine how Kyle would respond to *that*. Seemed to me like he'd just bite Ursula's head off. I could tell Blitz and Julian were thinking the same thing. We all looked at Anika to bail us out.

"Ursula, I don't think we should go the FLA route," Anika said carefully.

"Why NOT?" Ursula asked.

"Just trust me on this one," Anika said.

"But why NOT?" Ursula asked again. "I'm a good negotiator. You know, FLA sends out all these newsletters with lawyer tips, and I've read them *all*."

"That's...um...great," Anika said. "But I just don't think Kyle would be up for a negotiation like that. He'd probably see it as like being backed into a corner or pushed around or something. But I *do* think you're right about letting him know about the sneaker cleaner. I'll make sure to get the word out. That's probably the best way."

Ursula thought for a second.

"Okay," she said with a shrug. "If you think so."

Ursula always trusted Anika's opinion. That was one thing you could count on.

TRUST ME ON THIS ONE.

✳ ✳ ✳ ✳

Later that day, I ran into Anika in the hall.

"Well, bad news again," she said.

"What?" I asked.

"I made sure Kyle heard about the sneaker cleaner, but apparently he just laughed about it and said he'd believe *that* when he saw it."

"Predictable," I said, rolling my eyes.

"It's like I said," Anika explained. "He just wants to have somebody to pick on. Even if that person's, like, half his size."

"No kidding," I said.

Anika started to walk off, but then she turned and added something else:

"Oh, and I talked to Ursula, and I found out why she didn't want you guys to come over."

"Yeah, *and?*" I asked, really curious.

"Turns out she's had people over before, and they've said rude things about her grandma's cooking. They say it smells bad or something."

"Oh," I said. "That's not cool."

"I know," Anika said. "And she says her grandma doesn't speak all that much English, and she always offers people stuff to eat and feels bad if they don't like it."

"Well, we won't even be going inside," I said.

"I know," Anika said. "I just thought I'd give you the 411."

"Thanks," I said.

"No problem," she said. "I'll see you after school. Nervous?"

"Not at all," I said.

But of course I meant exactly the opposite.

And Anika knew it.

Right before school ended, we had Blitz walk past Kyle wearing his usual coat and the hat Julian would be wearing. (We wanted to make *sure* Kyle would be looking for *that* coat and *that* hat.)

GRRRRRRR

Then, when the bell rang, Julian, Blitz, and I dashed down the back stairs to the gym doors, which, just like Friday, were still open for us.

Again, we dashed across the gym.

And again, we waited behind the gym door, watching the crowd walk past.

But *this* time, unlike on Friday, we waited a little longer, both to give Ursula time to get home and to give the block a chance to clear out. We wanted to make *sure* Kyle and his friends saw Julian.

As we waited, Julian traded coats with Blitz and put on the wig and hat.

After what seemed like a loooong time, Julian finally gave us the nod.

"Okay," he said. "Ready or not..."

And Julian stepped out the door.

Blitz and I immediately ducked back from the door and plastered ourselves against the wall, since we didn't want Kyle and his friends to see us when they ran past.

Sure enough, about two seconds later, we heard:

"THERE HE IS!"

and

"HEY, YELLOWHEAD!"

About half a minute later, there was a knock on the gym door. I leaned out to have a look, and there was Anika giving us the "okay" sign.

Blitz and I quickly stepped outside, and the three of us started walking real fast to Blitz's place.

"Did it look like Julian got away?" I asked.

"Oh yeah," Anika said confidently. "That boy can *fly*. He was at least a block ahead of those guys when I saw him."

"Good," Blitz and I both said.

Anika walked with me and Blitz around the corner and two blocks north to Blitz's place. All three of us kept checking our rearview glasses to make sure Kyle and his friends hadn't given up and turned back. But they never appeared.

When we got to Blitz's place, Blitz was ready to celebrate.

"Mission accomplished!" he cheered. "We *totally* faked them out!"

"Yeah," I agreed, checking nervously in my rearview glasses. "But let's not stand around here. They know where you live, remember, and they could show up here once they lose Julian."

Blitz's eyes got wide again.

"You're right," he said, running up the stairs and opening his building door. Fortunately he had his key ready this time.

"See you guys tomorrow," he said.

And then he disappeared inside.

"I'll see *you* tomorrow, too," Anika said to me. "And be careful on the way to Ursula's."

"I will," I said with a smile.

✳ ✳ ✳ ✳

I took the long way to Ursula's place, since I didn't want to risk running into Kyle and company. When I got to Ursula's corner, I used my rearview glasses to look down the block.

Fortunately, the coast was clear.

So I ran down to Ursula's place and pressed the buzzer. Immediately the door buzzed open, so I stepped inside.

Julian wasn't waiting in the lobby, so I took the stairs up to Ursula's floor.

I expected to find Julian waiting in the hall, but he wasn't anywhere to be found. Weird. Maybe he'd left already?

I walked down the hall to Ursula's apartment, 3B. I'd never been to Ursula's place before. As I got closer, I could hear talking inside, a voice that was probably her grandmother's, speaking what I figured was Korean.

I knocked on the door, and Ursula almost immediately pulled it open.

"Hi, Spencer," she said.

And then I saw Ursula's grandmother in the background.

"Come in! Come in!" she said with a smile.

Ursula kind of smiled weakly and stepped aside so I could walk in. Inside, I saw Julian sitting at the kitchen table. He smiled and waved.

"Blitz got home safe?" Julian asked.

"Yup," I said. "And you didn't have any trouble outrunning those guys?"

"They didn't have a *chance*," Julian said. "I was inside Ursula's building before they even turned the corner."

"Excellent," I said. "I thought you were gonna wait in the hall?"

"He *was*," Ursula said. "But my grandma saw us. She walked past us on her way back from the laundry room."

"Oh," I said.

"Sit down," Ursula's grandma said to me, pointing at the kitchen table with a big smile. She seemed really nice.

But Ursula looked totally uncomfortable.

"She wants us to have a snack," Ursula said. "My grandma believes that you always offer guests something to eat."

"My grandma's the same way," Julian said.

"Really?" Ursula asked.

"Oh yeah," Julian said. "Right, Spencer?"

"Definitely," I agreed.

Julian lives with his grandma, and she's always offering me stuff to eat when I'm over there. She makes really good roast chicken and yellow rice. And fried bananas. It's kind of nice to eat there, since at my place we eat mostly takeout and leftovers of takeout.

Anyway, Ursula still looked uncomfortable as her grandmother placed three steaming bowls of noodles in front of us. They were big thick noodles. And the sauce smelled, well...different.

"You guys probably won't like it," Ursula said with a wince.

"I like noodles," Julian said.

"Me too," I nodded.

And we both started chowing down. The taste was definitely unlike anything I'd ever had before (kind of salty and a little bit tangy), but it wasn't bad. Just different.

And we ate it all. Every last bit.

Ursula's grandma looked really pleased. And I think Ursula was in shock. But she was definitely happy.

✱ ✱ ✱ ✱

After we finished our noodles, Julian and I thanked Ursula's grandmother, and we all walked downstairs.

"So you liked the noodles?" Ursula asked.

"Yeah," Julian said. "They were good."

"Some of my friends don't like my grandma's cooking," Ursula said. "That's why I wasn't sure you guys should even come in. 'Cause when people don't eat my grandma's cooking, she feels bad."

"I'd never do that," Julian said. "I know how grandmas can be."

It was kind of funny for me to hear Ursula and Julian actually *agreeing* about something for once.

I could tell they were thinking the same thing.

CHAPTER 7
THE BARKING TARANTULA

The next day after lunch, we all met in the school yard to talk about our totally excellent escape. But we couldn't congratulate ourselves for *too* long, because we had to figure out how we were going to get Blitz out *again* that day. And we knew the stakes were high, because Kyle and his friends were really revved up after two defeats in a row.

"Kyle purposely crashed into me in the hall this morning," Blitz reported. "Then he said, 'Oops, SORRY!' and crashed into me *again*. I just kept on walking."

"Good for you," Anika said.

"I could smell his breath. It was like rotten baloney," Blitz added.

ROTTEN BALONEY

"Oh, lovely," Anika said. "Thanks for sharing."

"Just warning you guys," Blitz said with a half-smile, half-grimace.

"Anyway," Ursula said, changing the subject. "My uncle said the sneaker cleaner's supposed to come in this morning. He said my cousin could bring it to my apartment at lunchtime, so maybe I can run home and get it right after school, then come back and be here with the peace offering just in case Kyle manages to catch you guys for once."

"He won't," Julian said confidently.

"But it's a good idea anyway," Anika nodded.

"Are we gonna do the decoy thing again?" Blitz asked Julian.

"We can if we need to," Julian said. "Guess we can just play it by ear."

"But I don't think you should use the gym exit again," Anika warned. "Kyle's definitely onto that. I've *heard.*"

"My thoughts exactly," Ursula agreed. "That's why I think you should use the *cafeteria* door. The one in the back."

Everyone's face lit up.

"Sweet!" Julian said. "You think the cafeteria ladies would let us use it?"

"Yup," Ursula said. "I talked to them this morning. I'll just go and remind them during last period."

"Cool," Blitz said. "Thanks."

"The only thing is, we'd have to use the main staircase to get down to the cafeteria," I said. "Kyle and those guys could see us if we don't time it right."

Everyone thought about that for a second.

"We'll just have to time it right, then," Julian said with a shrug. "I'll keep an eye out."

Everyone else nodded, so it seemed like we had a plan. I looked over at the court where Kyle and his friends always played basketball. I was expecting to see them in the middle of a game.

But instead, to my shock, they were looking right back at us.

✳ ✳ ✳ ✳

After school, Blitz came to meet me and Julian in our homeroom. We waited there for a few minutes till we thought Kyle and those guys were probably outside. We would've waited longer, but our homeroom teacher was kind of anxious for us to leave.

We stepped out into the hall and walked cautiously toward the main stairwell. But when we turned the corner, we were greeted by...well, a rather unpleasant surprise:

KYLE.

"Look who's here," Kyle said loudly.

And right then, Kyle's friends Eddie and Jake walked up and stood on either side of him.

Quickly, I pulled Blitz and Julian into the next open classroom: Mr. Lipsky's science room. I thought we'd be safe with a teacher around.

But Mr. Lipsky wasn't in there!

I was trying to think fast of somewhere else to go, when suddenly we heard...

"BOYS! TIME TO GO HOME! NOW!"

It was Mr. Naulty yelling at Kyle, Eddie, and Jake! For once, the sound of Mr. Naulty's voice was actually a *nice* thing.

"NOW! LET'S GO!"

"Okay, okay!"

"We're *going!*"

Kyle and his friends must've been moving really slowly down the hall, because then we heard Mr. Naulty blasting out:

"COME ON, BOYS! WE DON'T HAVE ALL DAY!"

They were being herded right out the door! PERFECT!

After about a minute, it seemed like the coast was clear, so we dashed down the main stairs.

We ran across the empty cafeteria to the door on the far side. And just as Ursula promised, it was open! Julian peeked outside.

"I think we're good to go," he said cautiously, looking in both directions. "Just wait a sec."

Julian and I both stepped outside to look around. It seemed quiet enough on the block.

But then I heard Blitz's voice from behind:

"Um...guys!"

And Julian and I both turned around to see, to our horror...

"RUN!" Julian and I both shouted, but it was too late. Kyle had already grabbed Blitz.

And he turned him UPSIDE DOWN!

Blitz's glasses fell off and stuff started pouring out of his backpack.

"PUT HIM DOWN!" Julian and I yelled.

But then Kyle's friends came over and got in our faces. Jake stood in front of Julian, and Eddie got in front of me.

After another second or two, Kyle kind of half-dropped Blitz on the sidewalk, and Blitz started hunting around for his glasses.

Julian and I were both trying to get away from Jake and Eddie so we could help Blitz, but then suddenly we all heard something strange. Something *very* strange, coming from Blitz's pocket:

Everyone stopped what they were doing and looked at Blitz's pocket.

"Do you have a DOG in your pocket, Yellowhead?" Kyle demanded.

"No," Blitz said in a tiny voice, finally finding his glasses and putting them on. "It's a tarantula."

"A WHAT?" Kyle asked, looming over Blitz's head.

"IT'S A TARANTULA," Blitz said, suddenly finding his voice somewhere.

Blitz pulled the thing out of his pocket—a little metal tarantula robot. It was still barking like crazy.

"And it BARKS?" Kyle asked.

"Yeah," Blitz said. "It gets set off by loud noises. See, it crawls fast, too."

Blitz set the tarantula down on the ground, and it crawled like mad toward Kyle's feet. *Man, that thing could really move!*

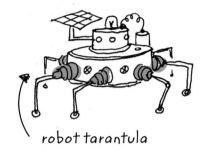

robot tarantula

When the tarantula got to Kyle's feet, it barked a couple of times and then turned around and went the other way.

"It avoids obstacles, too," Blitz explained.

Kyle nodded and picked the thing up.

"Thanks," he said, putting it in his pocket.

"HEY!" Blitz said. "That's mine."

"Go buy another," Kyle said.

"I didn't buy it," Blitz said.

"What, you *stole it?*" Kyle asked.

"No," Blitz said. "I *made it.*"

Kyle looked stunned. He took the tarantula out of his pocket and looked at it again.

"YOU MADE THIS?" he asked.

"Yeah," Blitz said quietly.

"He makes lots of stuff," I added.

"All *kinds* of gadgets," Julian said. "You name it, he can build it, more than you could even—"

I winced, because I knew where Julian was going, and I could only *imagine* how Kyle would react. But fortunately Julian couldn't finish, because he was interrupted by...

"Who's SHE?" Kyle demanded.

"That's Ursula," I said. "She has some cleaner to fix your shoe."

Kyle looked stunned. So did his friends.

"She has connections in the dry-cleaning industry," Blitz added.

"That's right," Ursula said, totally out of breath. "I got you the best sneaker cleaner on the *planet*. See?"

And she showed Kyle the label.

"Wanna try it?" Ursula asked Kyle.

Kyle shrugged.

"Fine," he grunted. I think he was still in shock.

So Ursula pulled a rag out of her pocket and squeezed some cleaner onto it, then knelt down and cleaned Kyle's shoe. We all leaned over and watched, waiting to see if the mark would really come off...

...and it did!

Kyle was speechless.

"Good as new!" Ursula said, stepping back. "Wanna clean your other one?"

"Sure," Kyle said, reaching for the cleaner.

After Kyle finished, his friends took turns using the cleaner, too. Ursula was all smiles.

"See," she said to me, Blitz, and Julian. "I told you this would work."

"Thanks," Blitz said quietly to Ursula. "I owe you one."

"We're not done yet," Ursula said. "We have to seal the deal."

And then she turned to Kyle and said, in her most down-to-business voice:

"So you're not gonna bother Blitz anymore, right? We have your word?"

Kyle shrugged and looked at the ground.

"If he stays outta my way," he said. "Like I said, I don't bother people who stay outta my way."

I didn't exactly remember Kyle saying anything like that recently, but whatever. It looked like everything was peachy. But then suddenly Julian spoke up...

"So give him back his tarantula," he said.

"HIS WHAT?" Ursula burst out in shock.

"My tarantula robot," Blitz explained. "Kyle has it. But it's okay."

"No it's NOT," Julian said. "It's your robot. He should give it back."

And then Julian said again to Kyle:

"Give him back his tarantula."

"Or what?" Kyle asked, stepping closer to Julian.

"HOLD ON A SECOND," Ursula said, stepping forward. "Let's negotiate like reasonable—"

"Back off," Kyle said, either to Julian or Ursula or both, I couldn't tell.

"Don't talk to her like that!" Julian said, stepping even closer to Kyle.

I was in shock. Julian was defending *Ursula*? This was completely new territory.

"I was talking to *you*," Kyle said to Julian.

"Guys, it really doesn't matter," Blitz tried to step in. "I have—"

But Blitz couldn't finish, because suddenly the door burst open, and out stepped...

"WHAT IS GOING ON HERE?" she demanded.

Everyone was silent.

"All of you, please come inside," she said, holding open the door. "Right now."

"School's over," Kyle grumbled.

"Yeah," Kyle's friends agreed.

"I don't care *what* time it is. These are school grounds, and this is a school problem," Miss Pryor said. "So we need to resolve this right now. So if you would please—"

But Miss Pryor couldn't finish, because suddenly, the door burst open and out stepped...

MR. NAULTY!

His face was the meanest I'd ever seen it.

"ALL OF YOU, INSIDE! NOW!" he roared.

Everyone stood there speechless.

"DON'T MAKE ME SAY IT AGAIN!" Mr. Naulty blasted. "NOW!"

And so we all marched inside.

CHAPTER 8
WRONG ANSWER

Inside, we all sat at one of the cafeteria tables, and we told the whole story to Miss Pryor and Mr. Naulty. Ursula, Blitz, Julian, and I did most of the talking.

Kyle and his friends mostly just sat there like three lumps, except to say a couple of times that they were totally right to be mad about the sneaker stain, and that the sneakers were expensive and new, and yadda yadda yadda.

But Ursula just shut them down every time by pointing out that the stained sneaker was now not only fine, but *better* than fine.

But Miss Pryor and Mr. Naulty weren't too interested in that part of it. They kept talking about the fact that we should have come to them for help.

"No one should EVER have to be afraid for their safety at school OR after school," Miss Pryor insisted. "If you EVER feel threatened again, I want you to come to me, or Mr. Naulty, or one of the other teachers. Do you understand?"

We all nodded...except Blitz.

"But that doesn't always help," Blitz argued.

"Of course it does," Mr. Naulty insisted.

Everyone was silent. But Blitz spoke up again.

"But then you get a reputation for being a tattletale," Blitz said.

"And a wuss," Julian pointed out.

"And then they *never* leave you alone," Blitz argued. "I know, 'cause that was the story of my LIFE in fourth grade."

"How did you solve the problem back in fourth grade?" Miss Pryor asked.

"Just by ignoring them and doing my own thing," Blitz said with a shrug. "Till finally they gave up."

"That's a good strategy," Miss Pryor said. "But if it gets out of hand, you should know when to ask for help."

"I'm telling you," Blitz said, shaking his head. "It's *complicated*."

"We know," Miss Pryor said. "And that's why no one ever has to know you came to us. Just quietly tell us there's a problem, and we can step in and help. Like today—I'm sure none of you know how we found out about this situation today."

We all shook our heads.

"How *did* you find out?" Ursula asked.

"That's not important," Mr. Naulty said gruffly.

"We're aware of more than you think," Miss Pryor said. "Give us some credit."

"Anyway," Mr. Naulty said, changing the subject suddenly, "this problem better be OVER, as of NOW."

We all looked down at the table.

"I'm especially disappointed that you kids would act up during such an *important* time," Mr. Naulty continued, shaking his head.

I immediately knew he was talking about the BRM test coming up, since that was ALL Mr. Naulty EVER talked about these days. It was only two weeks away.

But I could tell from the blank looks on Kyle, Eddie, and Jake's faces that they had no idea what Mr. Naulty was talking about. And unfortunately, Mr. Naulty could tell, too.

"You *do* know what I'm talking about, don't you?" Mr. Naulty demanded, looking at Kyle and company with laser eyes.

Kyle, Eddie, and Jake looked down at the table with glowering faces. They didn't say a word.

"I'm talking about the BRM test," Mr. Naulty said sternly. "The test that will decide whether or not YOU will be promoted this year. And if I were you, I would NOT be taking that lightly right now. Do you understand me?"

Kyle and his friends still sat there in angry silence.

"Do you understand how important this test is?" Miss Pryor asked them again, in a nicer voice than Mr. Naulty's.

I DON'T CARE ABOUT THAT STUPID TEST!

And that's when Kyle suddenly looked up and blurted out:

"I don't care about that stupid test!"

"Me neither," Eddie agreed.

"Yeah, who cares," Jake added.

Well, needless to say, that was the **wrong answer**.

 Mr. Naulty looked like his temperature had just gone up to about five million degrees.

 Miss Pryor looked like her dog had just died.

 Ursula looked like her eyes were about to pop out of her head.

 And Julian, Blitz, and I just waited for the explosion we knew was coming...

"NOT ACCEPTABLE!" Mr. Naulty blasted, slamming his fist on the table. "THAT ATTITUDE IS NOT ACCEPTABLE!"

"I don't care," Kyle said.

"You HAVE to care," Mr. Naulty said.

"I SAID I don't care," Kyle said *again*, digging himself even deeper into the hole. Was he trying to get to China? Sure seemed like it.

"If THAT is your attitude, Kyle," Mr. Naulty said, barely able to contain himself, "then I have no choice..."

Mr. Naulty paused for a moment, and we all waited to hear what exactly he had no choice about. Finally he spoke:

"You'll spend your lunch period upstairs for the next two weeks, and during that time, you will LEARN about the importance of this test."

Julian, Ursula, Blitz, and I all gasped. Two weeks' worth of lunch periods spent on the BRM test? That was a fate worse than DEATH, if you ask me.

"That's not FAIR!" Kyle protested. "You can't take away my LUNCH!"

"You'll eat your lunch upstairs," Mr. Naulty said. "And after that, your teachers will *personally* help you prepare for the test."

Miss Pryor nodded solemnly.

"All three of you," Mr. Naulty added. "You can learn not only about the test, but also why we should not BULLY OTHERS. Sounds to me like an *excellent* use of your lunch period."

"**NO!**" Kyle, Eddie, and Jake all shouted at once.

Ooh! That was rough. We all *knew* how much Kyle, Jake, and Eddie liked playing basketball during our free time after lunch.

"I'm sorry," Mr. Naulty said, "but that's how it's going to be. We're going upstairs right now to call your parents, and I'm sure they'll support the idea."

Kyle, Eddie, and Jake looked like they were ready to throw tantrums right there on the cafeteria floor.

"But that's not FAIR!" Eddie yelled.

But Mr. Naulty wasn't hearing any of it.

"End of discussion," he said. "Another word, and I'll add an after-school session, too. And I mean it."

Jake, Eddie, and Kyle just glared silently at Mr. Naulty. After that, Mr. Naulty made them all go upstairs with him to call their parents. The rest of us walked to the cafeteria exit with Miss Pryor.

"Well, I hope we've resolved this problem," Miss Pryor said to Blitz on the way to the door. "I think they'll leave you alone now."

"Hope so," Blitz said with a shrug.

"Kyle still has his robot," Julian pointed out.

"It's okay," Blitz said quickly. "He can have it if he wants it so much."

"But it's YOURS," Julian insisted.

"But he can have it," Blitz said. "I don't care."

"But it's the *principle* of the matter," Ursula insisted.

"Well, it's up to Nathan, isn't it?" Miss Pryor asked Ursula.

It was always funny when people used Blitz's real name.

"He can have the robot," Blitz said firmly. "As a peace offering. I have lots of other ones."

"That's a very nice gesture," Miss Pryor said with a smile. "I'll make sure he knows."

HE CAN HAVE THE ROBOT... AS A PEACE OFFERING.

CAFETERIA

"I can't *believe* you let that loser have your tarantula," Julian said to Blitz, once we were outside.

"I don't need it anymore," Blitz said. "That was the beta version."

"The what?" Julian asked.

"The beta version," Blitz repeated. "The test model. Normally I'd use the parts for scrap, but I have *plenty* of scrap. And I've already moved way beyond that old stuff."

And Blitz reached into his backpack and pulled out *another* tarantula.

"This is the latest model," he said. "This one can climb walls. *And* it glows in the dark."

"COOL!" Julian said, looking at the new tarantula.

"And this one doesn't bark," Blitz added. "It *roars*."

Blitz switched the thing on and clapped his hands. And sure enough, the thing roared. Loud. Nice!

CHAPTER 9
JUSTICE IS SWEET

Instead of going straight home that day, we all stopped by Blitz's place to look at his robot collection. It was totally cool.

Blitz also showed us his latest "get out of bed on time" contraption: The Evictor.

"That's how I've been getting to school on time these days," Blitz said. "When the alarm goes off, the right side of the bed starts lifting and lifting till finally I can't stay in there anymore. Works like a charm."

THE EVICTOR

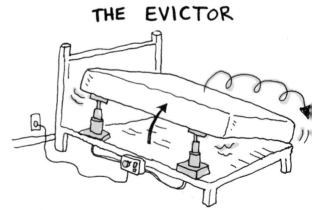

We all shook our heads in disbelief.

"Wow," Julian said.

Blitz was explaining to us how the mechanics worked when his phone rang and he ran to get it.

"Guys!" he called from the kitchen. "It's Anika!"

So we all ran out there, and Blitz put Anika on the speaker-phone so we could all hear.

"*There* you guys are," she said. "I was worried sick."

"We're okay," I said. "There was almost trouble, but then Miss Pryor and Mr. Naulty stepped in."

"I know," Anika said.

"You *know?*" Ursula asked. "How?"

"'Cause *I'm* the one who sent them," Anika said.

"YOU DID?" Blitz asked.

"Yeah," Anika said. "I was watching from the third floor window to make sure there wasn't any trouble, and I saw Kyle come out holding Blitz upside down..."

"He held you UPSIDE DOWN?" Ursula asked Blitz, her eyes wide.

Blitz nodded.

"So I ran and got Miss Pryor," Anika continued, "and then I thought I'd better throw in Mr. Naulty, too, just in case."

"Good call," I said.

"So everything's okay?" Anika asked.

SO I RAN AND GOT MISS PRYOR, AND THEN I THOUGHT I'D BETTER THROW IN MR. NAULTY, TOO, JUST IN CASE.

"Oh yeah," Julian said. "They won't mess with us anymore."

"They're in *huge* trouble," Ursula said. "They have to stay inside during lunch and do test prep. For two weeks!"

"Ooh!" Anika said. "Harsh!"

"It's *almost* cruel and unusual punishment," Ursula said.

"Nah," Julian said. "It's justice."

"Totally," Blitz agreed.

✹ ✹ ✹ ✹

The next day after lunch, sure enough, Kyle's basketball court was empty.

"And don't look now," Anika said. "But they're looking out the window."

"Which window?" Ursula asked urgently.

"Don't everybody look at once," Anika said. "Miss Pryor's window."

After a couple seconds, I casually looked up there, and sure enough, there they were, looking down at the school yard. They looked totally depressed.

"Looks like they're hard at work," Ursula said sarcastically.

"Well, hopefully they'll get *something* done," Anika said. "I hope they don't fail the BRM."

"Who cares if they do?" Julian asked.

"*I* care," Anika said.

We all looked at her with wide eyes.

"Didn't you know that the test results are put out in the newspaper, and the school gets a ranking based on them?" Anika asked.

We all shrugged. I think I *kind of* knew that, but I hadn't thought about it much because I didn't really care.

"Well, my parents keep talking about taking me out of this school," Anika said. "And if the school gets a bad ranking, they might."

We all got quiet.

"Really?" Ursula asked.

"Yeah," Anika said. "This school used to be one of the top schools, but it's been sliding downhill these past few years. My parents keep talking about taking me out, but I keep telling them that things are shaping up, thanks to all the cool stuff we've been doing. But if the test scores are bad, that might be *it*."

We all winced. It was hard to imagine school without Anika.

"My mom's been saying stuff like that, too," Blitz said.

We all winced again. I bet if my parents knew more about my school, they'd be saying the same thing. But my mom's too busy at work, and my dad's too far away.

"Well, anyway," Anika said. "I don't mean to depress everybody."

"People *better* do well on that test," I said. "We've been prepping for it so much, I think I could take it in my *sleep*."

"Me too," Blitz agreed, and the others nodded.

"Yeah," Ursula said. "I have that thing *down*. I don't want to devote another single brain cell to it."

"Exactly," Julian said, turning to me and Blitz. "Anyone wanna play basketball? There's a free court, obviously."

Blitz and I both nodded.

"You guys have fun," Ursula said. "I have a business to run."

"What business?" Anika asked. "I thought the smoothie thing was on Fridays."

"I'm starting a *new* business," Ursula explained. "Sneaker cleaning. Fifty cents a pair."

And we all watched in amazement as Ursula took a sign from her bag, folded it in half like a tent, and set it on the ground. Then she got out her bottle of sneaker cleaner and a cloth.

"Any of you want a cleaning?" she asked. "Ooh, Spencer, looks like you need one."

"Do I get a discount?" I asked.

"Of course not," Ursula said. Then she smiled and added: "This one's on the house."

"Thanks," I said, even though I didn't exactly care if my sneakers looked new or not. Guess I have a different opinion on sneakers than most guys at my school.

"And you know where my profits are going to go, after I pay for the cleaner?" Ursula asked.

"Where?" Julian asked.

"To Blitz," Ursula said proudly. "'Cause he had to pay for the wig. I think he should have his money back so he can keep doing the stuff he does best."

"Wow, thanks!" Blitz said with bright eyes. Then he grinned and added: "I'll name my next robot 'Ursula' if you want. Or maybe the 'Ursu-bot'!"

Ursula looked kind of horrified.

"Um, that's okay," she said. "But thanks."

And so I got my sneakers cleaned up like new, and so did Blitz. And pretty soon, Ursula was in business.

And I'm happy to report, business was good.

CHAPTER 10
THE MATHINATOR

Ursula had at least four days of steady good business, but then, unfortunately, the teachers caught on and she got shut down for running an "unauthorized business on school grounds." Ursula tried to argue that it was no different from her smoothie stand, but the teachers pointed out that all the profits from the smoothie stand went to the school, which was true. So Ursula had to admit defeat.

But fortunately, she'd already made enough to pay her uncle back for the sneaker cleaner, and to give Blitz $21.50 to *almost* pay him back for the wig. If only we could've returned the wig, we would've made a huge profit on the whole operation. But the Masquerade Market has a no-return policy on wigs—I guess 'cause of head lice and personal germs and stuff like that. Oh well.

Anyway, I would've thought that would have been the end of this operation, but then Blitz did something that surprised everybody. And I'm not just talking about the rest of us Spy Fives. I mean *everybody*.

* * * *

"Guess what?" Blitz said one day after lunch, about a week after the big showdown in the cafeteria. "I thought of a way to help out Kyle and those guys."

"YOU WANT TO HELP THEM OUT?" Ursula blasted.

"Well, it's kind of like helping myself, too," Blitz said. "I figure if I help them out, then they'll definitely never bother me again. *And* my idea will help a lot of other people, too."

We were all intrigued.

"What's your idea?" I asked.

"The Mathinator," Blitz said. "I invented it last weekend."

"The MATHINATOR?" Ursula asked. "What's it do?"

"It's a way to prepare for the math part of the BRM test while playing basketball," Blitz explained, pulling out a spiral notebook with the Mathinator shown inside. "You see a math question up here, and you dunk the ball in the hoop where the right answer is showing. It's all timed, so you have to answer ten questions before the buzzer goes off. And I made the baskets just the right height for kids to dunk."

We all looked at the thing in stunned silence.

from Blitz's notebook

"Whoa," Julian said. "How'd you think of *that*?"

"It just sort of came to me," Blitz said with a shrug. "I'm always like that. Whenever I see a problem, I can't stop thinking about it till I think of a way to solve it. And then when I think of a way to solve it, I have to see if I can actually build it. And so I start building it, and then I can't stop till I make it work. I guess you could call me obsessed."

"No," Anika said, shaking her head with a smile. "I'd call you *ingenious*."

Blitz looked embarrassed. But he kept explaining.

"In this case, I was thinking, there's gotta be a way to do test prep that's not painful. 'Cause test prep is actually a *good* thing— I mean, anything that helps people pass that test and not get left back is a good thing. There just has to be a better way to do it. You know, like a spoonful of sugar helps the medicine go down."

"I like the way you think," Anika said.

"And you've already built this thing?" I asked.

"Yup," Blitz said. "Last weekend. I've been testing it out at home. I can set it up here tomorrow."

"Wow, Blitz," Ursula said. "You've *really* outdone yourself this time. I'm in shock."

And everyone else nodded in agreement.

* * * *

So, the next day, Blitz got permission from the teachers to set up the Mathinator in the school yard. They were just as amazed by the idea as we were. Even Mr. Naulty was impressed.

Miss Pryor gave Kyle and company special permission to try out the machine. And of course, they were totally grateful.

It was a pretty amazing thing to watch, I have to say. They actually got better and better and faster and faster at answering the questions.

So it looked like Blitz's creation really *did* help those guys out. A lot. And like Anika said (and like Blitz said, too)—anything that helps *them* helps *us*, if you make yourself think about it that way.

✳ ✳ ✳ ✳

So anyway, that about wraps up this operation. I'm happy to say, we all took the BRM test last week. So it's over with. Out of our hair. DONE!

Of course, we won't know how we all did for another two months or so, but everyone *I've* talked to thought the test was a snap. And how do you think we all feel?

A) Like it's the first warm day after a loooooong winter

B) Like a huge weight has been lifted off our shoulders

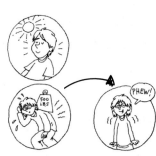

C) Like we won some kind of extra-long marathon

D) Like we're on top of the world

E) All of the above

And if you picked E, well, you got it!

Until next time, *Spencer*

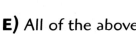

Spy Gear Manual

Rearview Glasses and Spy Five Cap

Sneak a peek behind you!

Throw on a quick disguise!

What Can You Spy with Your Rearview Eyes?

Wear your rearview glasses at the park, in a movie theater (before the movie starts), or on a bus, train, or subway. Watch the people behind you. When people don't realize they're being watched, they'll act more naturally and talk more normally. Try it—you can see and hear some pretty unusual stuff!

Try a Quick Change

A disguise doesn't have to involve a wig or fancy makeup or anything like that. Just a quick change is all you need sometimes. Try this!

1. Wear two thin jackets, one on top of the other, and put your Spy Five cap and your rearview glasses in your pocket.

REARVIEW GLASSES IN POCKET

CAP IN POCKET

2. Go to a crowded park or playground with a friend, and tell your friend you're going to play hide-and-seek.

   When your friend turns around to count, do a quick change: Swap your jackets (put the inside jacket on the outside) and put on your cap. Slip on your rearview glasses, too.

The Real Deal!

Real spies use the quick-change technique to lose someone who's trying to follow them.

   Sometimes they'll even wear a reversible jacket or carry an extra hat so they're ready!

3. Move into a crowded area, and make sure your back is facing your friend. Don't make eye contact (you can watch your friend with your rearview glasses). How long does it take your friend to find you? Probably longer than you'd think!

Have fun with the quick change ...and try more wise disguises, too!

— Spencer